TAYLOR LAUTNER

Amie Jane Leavitt

Mitchell Lane
PUBLISHERS

P.O. Box 196
Hockessin, Delaware 19707
Visit us on the web: www.mitchelllane.com
Comments? email us: mitchelllane@mitchelllane.com

Copyright © 2011 by Mitchell Lane Publishers. All rights reserved. No part of this book may be reproduced without written permission from the publisher. Printed and bound in the United States of America.

Printing   1   2   3   4   5   6   7   8   9

A Robbie Reader
Contemporary Biography

Abigail Breslin	Albert Pujols	Alex Rodriguez
Aly and AJ	Amanda Bynes	AnnaSophia Robb
Ashley Tisdale	Brenda Song	Brittany Murphy
Charles Schulz	Dakota Fanning	Dale Earnhardt Jr.
David Archuleta	Demi Lovato	Donovan McNabb
Drake Bell & Josh Peck	Dr. Seuss	Dwayne "The Rock" Johnson
Dylan & Cole Sprouse	Eli Manning	Emily Osment
Emma Watson	Hilary Duff	Jaden Smith
Jamie Lynn Spears	Jennette McCurdy	Jesse McCartney
Jimmie Johnson	Johnny Gruelle	Jonas Brothers
Jordin Sparks	Justin Bieber	Keke Palmer
Larry Fitzgerald	LeBron James	Mia Hamm
Miley Cyrus	Miranda Cosgrove	Raven-Symoné
Selena Gomez	Shaquille O'Neal	Story of Harley-Davidson
Syd Hoff	**Taylor Lautner**	Tiki Barber
Tom Brady	Tony Hawk	Victoria Justice

Library of Congress Cataloging-in-Publication Data
Leavitt, Amie Jane.
  Taylor Lautner / by Amie Jane Leavitt.
      p. cm. — (A Robbie reader)
  Includes bibliographical references and index.
  Includes filmography and webliography.
  ISBN 978-1-58415-897-4 (library bound)
  1. Lautner, Taylor, 1992– —Juvenile literature. 2. Actors—United States
Biography—Juvenile literature. I. Title.
PN2287.L2855L43 2010
791.4302'8092—dc22
[B]
                                                                                           2010008961

ABOUT THE AUTHOR: Amie Jane Leavitt is an accomplished author and photographer. She graduated from Brigham Young University as an education major and has since taught all subjects and grade levels in both private and public schools. She is an adventurer who loves to travel the globe in search of interesting story ideas and beautiful places to capture on film. She has written dozens of books for kids, including *Victoria Justice* for Mitchell Lane Publishers. Amie enjoys writing about people who are achieving their dreams. For this reason, she particularly enjoyed researching and writing this book on Taylor Lautner.

PUBLISHER'S NOTE: The following story has been thoroughly researched and to the best of our knowledge represents a true story. While every possible effort has been made to ensure accuracy, the publisher will not assume liability for damages caused by inaccuracies in the data, and makes no warranty on the accuracy of the information contained herein. This story has not been authorized or endorsed by Taylor Lautner.

TABLE OF CONTENTS

Chapter One
A New Moon 5

Chapter Two
The Karate Kid 9

Chapter Three
Sharkboy 15

Chapter Four
Twilight 19

Chapter Five
Shooting for the Moon 25

Chronology 28
Filmography 29
Find Out More 30
    Articles 30
    Works Consulted 30
    Videos 30
Glossary 31
Index 32

Words in **bold** type can be found in the glossary.

In July 2009, Taylor appeared at Comic-Con International with his costars from the *Twilight* series. Thousands of fans descended on the convention, hoping to get a chance to see their favorite stars.

CHAPTER ONE

A New Moon

Days before the annual **Comic-Con International** (in-ter-NASH-uh-nul), more than 12,000 people camped on the lawn of the San Diego **Convention** (kun-VEN-shun) Center. They sweated in the sun and slept in sleeping bags and tents. They hoped to be one of the lucky fans to get to see the stars of *Twilight* in person.

On the day of the event, the fans screamed wildly. The noise was so loud, it sounded more like a rock concert than a film discussion.

"Comic-Con was crazy," Taylor Lautner told a reporter after the event. "Just coming

CHAPTER ONE

out onstage and hearing everyone scream and seeing how many people were in that auditorium was crazy."

The fans were allowed to ask the stars questions about the movie and the books. Taylor answered a question about his role in the film: "Jacob goes through a lot in this movie—he **transforms** mentally and emotionally. The most challenging for me was physically, so I had a lot of hard work cut out for me

Taylor sits with his costars Kristen Stewart and Robert Pattinson for a question-and-answer session with the fans of *New Moon*. During Comic-Con, they did 52 online and radio interviews and 25 television interviews.

after filming *Twilight*. I worked really hard to transform Jacob's body so I could portray him correctly for all you guys. And I hope you guys are pleased when you see the results."

The fans screamed wildly in approval. They liked Taylor in the first movie, but now he had definitely transformed into a smooth, confident movie star. Even his costars noticed how he reacted to the fans. "He's much better at doing it [than I am]," Robert Pattinson told *Vanity Fair*. "He's completely handling it. I'm just freaking out all the time. I'm going to end up . . . looking like an idiot."

The fans at Comic-Con were overjoyed at seeing the stars in person. But they still had to wait another four months before they would get to see *New Moon* on the big screen. It wouldn't be released until November 2009.

Taylor plays a shapeshifting wolf in *New Moon*

In May 2008, Taylor and his sister, Makena, attended the Los Angeles premiere of *Cheaper by the Dozen 2*. Taylor played the role of Eliot Murtaugh in this film.

CHAPTER TWO

The Karate Kid

Taylor Daniel Lautner was born on February 11, 1992, in Grand Rapids, Michigan. He was an only child for six and a half years, until his sister, Makena, was born in the fall of 1998.

Taylor's father, Daniel, is a pilot for a **commercial** (kuh-MER-shul) **airline**. His mother, Deb Lautner, was a project manager for Herman Miller—an office equipment company in the Grand Rapids area.

Since both of Taylor's parents worked, he spent his days before elementary school in day care. "I was a biter at day care," Taylor told a Grand Rapids newspaper reporter in October

CHAPTER TWO

2008. "I don't remember it, but my parents tell me I'd bite other kids." It's funny that years later he'd get a role in a vampire movie playing a teen who **morphs** into a snarling wolf with sharp, snapping teeth. He seems to have been a perfect fit for the role from a very young age.

One night, when Taylor was four years old, his dad was out of town on an overnight flight. Taylor's aunt invited him and his mom to stay at her house. During the night, their phone rang. "The police called and told us our house had burned down," Taylor said. Of course, they were crushed by the news, but they were grateful for their safety. "If my aunt hadn't invited us to sleep over . . . well, wow," he told *The Grand Rapids Press* in October 2008.

The family moved fifteen miles to the west, to the small town of Hudsonville, where several of his aunts and uncles lived. Taylor would call Hudsonville home until the age of eleven. While there, he attended public school at Jamestown Elementary.

Taylor has been a sports fanatic practically from birth. He especially loves wrestling,

THE KARATE KID

Taylor still enjoys playing sports. In February 2010, he joined other celebrities in the Fourth Annual Celebrity Beach Bowl in South Beach, Florida. Taylor was on the team coached by Mark Sanchez, quarterback for the New York Jets.

football, baseball, and basketball. At the age of six, he started taking karate lessons at Fabiano's Karate in the nearby town of Holland.

Taylor loved karate and spent a lot of his spare time training. At age seven, he attended

CHAPTER TWO

Taylor wows the crowd at the 2005 premiere of *Sahara*. His first karate instructor, Tom Fabiano, told *The Grand Rapids Press*, "A lot of boys that age are bouncing off the walls, but Taylor was always deliberate, focused. He wasn't a typical kid. He always worked extra hard."

his first national karate tournament and won three first-place trophies. While there, he also met someone who would be very important in his life: karate trainer Mike Chat.

Mike's specialty was extreme karate, which included stunts and flips. Mike invited Taylor to a karate camp. When he attended, "I fell in love [with the sport]," Taylor told *The Grand Rapids Press*. "By the end of the camp, I was doing aerial cartwheels with no hands."

Mike invited Taylor to join Team Chat International. Taylor would fly out to Los Angeles and train with Mike. Then he would fly home on a red-eye (overnight) flight and go to school the next day. This training became very tiring, but it "set me up for my life," he said in a *Rolling Stone* interview. "It gave me the **confidence**, the **discipline** and the hard work. Chat used to tell me, 'If you don't give 110 percent, you are not going to get anywhere.'"

All of Taylor's hard work eventually paid off. By the age of eleven, Taylor was a four-time world champion in extreme martial arts.

In *The Adventures of Sharkboy and Lavagirl 3D*, Taylor costarred with another actor who had the same first name as him. In this movie, Taylor Dooley plays the role of Lavagirl. This wouldn't be the only time this would happen to Taylor. In 2010, he would play in the movie *Valentine's Day* with singer Taylor Swift.

CHAPTER THREE

Sharkboy

Karate wasn't the only reason Taylor kept **commuting** to Los Angeles. Mike Chat had also encouraged him to get involved in acting. Taylor and his parents were "scared at first," Taylor told *Rolling Stone*. "We were like, 'No, that's not for us.' I was like, 'I'm sticking to my sports.' But for some reason, this guy believed in me. He said he'd put us up at his house for a month. And he'd help get me on **auditions**."

After several years of long-distance commuting, the family decided to move to Los Angeles (L.A.). "It was a big deal to leave," Taylor told a newspaper reporter in 2008. "All our family was here [in Michigan]." Yet, even

CHAPTER THREE

though his uncles, aunts, and cousins would miss him, they knew it was the best decision. Taylor's grandfather said, "He needs to get out there in L.A. You know, he needs to take a shot at this stuff."

In 2003, Taylor and his family packed their bags and moved.

Settling into L.A. life wasn't easy. Taylor auditioned, auditioned, and auditioned. "I heard no, no, no, no, so many times," he said—but he kept on trying.

Over the first few months, he landed small roles in commercials and television programs. Then his big break came in 2004 when he was chosen to play the part of Sharkboy in *The Adventures of Sharkboy and Lavagirl 3D*. "Oh, we freaked out," Taylor told *The Grand Rapids Press* in October 2008. "My whole family couldn't sleep for, like, a week."

Taylor liked working with the other actors and doing fun stuff on the set of this movie. He had to have a good imagination to perform in this film, because 90 percent of it was done in front of a plain green screen. The computer images would be placed into the movie later on.

He also said that it was tough doing schoolwork. He would shoot a portion of a scene, then go study with his tutor for a few minutes, then be called back to shoot. It was difficult switching back and forth.

When the director found out Taylor had a background in karate, he asked him to use his imagination and put together a martial arts fight scene all by himself. Taylor did flips and stunts, and then the computer people inserted the cartoon characters later on. Creating that scene was one of Taylor's favorite parts of the movie.

In 2005, Taylor landed the role of Eliot Murtaugh in *Cheaper by the Dozen 2*. He particularly enjoyed working with funnyman Steve Martin. During the filming of this movie, he told reporter Terri Finch Hamilton in 2008, "I stopped looking at movie stars as movie stars, and just looked at them as people."

Taylor had to wear a long black wig for his role as Jacob in the *Twilight* series. It was hot and itchy and sometimes awkward to wear. When a reporter for *The Examiner* asked him in 2009 if he was going to keep it, he replied, "If you give it to me I'll probably burn it."

CHAPTER FOUR

Twilight

In November 2007, Taylor got a call from his agent about a new movie called *Twilight*. Taylor had never heard of it before, but his agent insisted that he audition for the part of Jacob Black. "You really want this—it's a big one," he said.

The casting directors wanted to cast a Native American in the role since the character was a member of the Quileute (KOY-oot) tribe. Even though Taylor is of mainly French, Dutch, and German descent (with only a little Native American blood), they still decided he was the best man for the part.

CHAPTER FOUR

In order to prepare for his role in the film, Taylor actually met with teenagers from the Quileute tribe. "We went out to dinner with them and got a chance to talk to them. The funny thing I learned is that they're just like me."

The film was enormously successful. It earned $70 million in its first three days and has since made more than $400 million. Taylor enjoyed working with all of the members of the *Twilight* cast and said that they're all really close. He told *Interview* magazine, "It would be difficult for our characters if we weren't. It's a love triangle, and we need to understand each other." Taylor was in only five scenes in the movie, but he knew he'd have a much bigger role in the **sequel**, *New Moon*. First, he had to guarantee his spot in that film.

The casting directors weren't sure if they'd have Taylor continue to play the part of Jacob. In *New Moon*, Jacob is supposed to be a big muscular guy, but Taylor was still young and thin.

Taylor spent eleven months on a strict diet, avoiding sweets and bulking up. He'd need strength and lean muscle to play Jacob in *New Moon*. The film's director, Chris Weitz, told *Entertainment Weekly* in 2009, "People have seen [Taylor's] body and . . . it's a shocker because it's hard to believe that anyone can be quite so carved. But he actually delivers a really great performance. He wasn't just exercising all day, he was also reading the book."

CHAPTER FOUR

The day after they finished filming *Twilight*, Taylor hired a personal trainer and spent five days a week, several hours a day, in the gym. The hardest part wasn't exercising. It was eating big meals every two hours so that he could build muscle.

At the end of his training, he had gained thirty-two pounds of muscle and guaranteed himself the role of Jacob in *New Moon*. Not only did Taylor now have the right look, he could also do stunts. "Taylor did every single stunt that he could possibly get his hands on," director Chris Weitz said at Comic-Con in 2009. "Really, if Jacob is doing something impressive in the film, it's pretty much Taylor doing it."

This movie really pushed Taylor into stardom. Wherever he and his cast mates go, **paparazzi** (pah-pah-RAHT-zee) follow them and girls scream out their names. Taylor definitely loves his fans. He knows they feel very strongly about the *Twilight* books, movies, and characters. "We've met many different fans: the criers, who come around quite often; the

TWILIGHT

Twilight fans divide themselves into two groups; Team Jacob and Team Edward. These fans are obviously Team Jacob supporters. Despite Taylor's instant fame, he has managed to stay close with his family and friends. He tries to keep his acting career in the right perspective.

hyperventilators (hy-per-VEN-tih-lay-turz) who stop breathing and have to have a medic come. We've definitely seen some passion," Taylor told Michael Martin for *Interview* magazine.

It's difficult for young people to stay grounded when they are suddenly huge movie stars. Fortunately for Taylor, he has good friends and family who help him keep his feet on the ground.

Taylor likes to help others. In January 2009, he participated in the Lollipop Theater Network Fundraiser with actress Vanessa Anne Hudgens of *High School Musical*. This nonprofit organization gives children in hospitals the chance to see new releases of movies.

CHAPTER FIVE

Shooting for the Moon

Taylor is lucky to come from a family that is very down-to-earth and has good solid values. Not every celebrity has that. From the time Taylor was young, he went to church (Catholic) with his family. He was also taught the importance of hard work. Taylor's parents have insisted that he be responsible with the money he is making. They encourage him to put it in the bank and not buy things that are really expensive.

Another way Taylor stays grounded is by spending time with family and friends. When he visits Michigan, he still likes to do the same

CHAPTER FIVE

things he did before he became a big star. "I go fishing with one set of grandparents, I go quad riding with the other set. We go trap shooting. It's so much fun."

Since the *Twilight* craze started, he's been followed almost around the clock by paparazzi. One of the jobs of these photographers is to catch celebrities doing crazy things. Taylor told *Rolling Stone* magazine in December 2009, "They probably get annoyed, because I don't do [crazy] things. When I'm at home, I wake up, I go to the gym. I get in my car. I drive down to L.A., and I go to meetings all day. Then I come back, eat dinner, see my family, see friends, go to bed, and then do the same thing over again the next day." Taylor tries to live up to the standards that his family has taught him and tries to make good moral choices with his life. He likes to have fun, but he likes to do so in a good, clean way.

Taylor enjoys helping other people through charity work. In 2009, he participated in the Lollipop Theater Network, which brings hit movies to kids in hospitals. He also helped out with a reading program called Books for Kids Foundation.

Meanwhile, he wants to continue acting. In 2010, he was looking forward to his roles in *Stretch Armstrong, Abduction, Cancun,* and *Max Steel,* as well as the next two films in the *Twilight* series, *Eclipse* and *Breaking Dawn.* In 2009, he started a production company with his father (Tailor Made Entertainment) and is planning to make many different types of films and television shows. Taylor loves acting, but he can also see himself screenwriting and directing someday, too.

With Taylor's positive outlook on life, sparkling smile, handsome good looks, and strong work ethic, he is sure to be a success in whatever he decides to do. Fans of Team Jacob, of course, hope that he continues acting for many, many years to come. And if Taylor has anything to say about it, he definitely will.

CHRONOLOGY

1992 Taylor Daniel Lautner is born on February 11.

1996 His house burns down in Grand Rapids, Michigan. The family moves to Hudsonville, Michigan.

1998 His sister, Makena, is born. He begins taking karate lessons at Fabiano's Karate in Holland, Michigan.

1999 He attends a regional karate championship in Louisville, Kentucky. He wins three first-place titles. He meets Mike Chat, future extreme karate instructor. He attends Mike's karate camp at the University of California–Los Angeles.

2000 He joins Team Chat International. He wins his first three championship medals. He begins traveling back and forth to L.A. for karate and acting auditions.

2001 He is booked in a promotional spot for Nickelodeon's *Rugrats*. He lands a small part in the TV movie *Shadow Fury*.

2003 He moves with his family from Michigan to Los Angeles, California. He begins learning jazz and hip-hop and joins a hip-hop dance group called L.A. Hip Kids.

2004 He gets small roles in television shows such as *My Wife and Kids*, *The Bernie Mac Show*, *Summerland*, and *The Nick & Jessica Variety Hour*.

2005 He gets small roles in *Cheaper by the Dozen 2*; *Danny Phantom*; *Duck Dodgers*; and *What's New, Scooby-Doo?*; and the lead role of Sharkboy in *The Adventures of Sharkboy and Lavagirl 3-D*.

2006 He is the voice of the bully in *He's a Bully, Charlie Brown*. He is nominated for a Young Artist Award for the Best Performance in a Feature Film for *The Adventures of Sharkboy and Lavagirl 3-D*.

2008 He plays the part of Jack Spivey in the television show *My Own Worst Enemy*. He plays the part of Jacob Black in *Twilight*.

2009 He plays the part of Jacob Black in *The Twilight Saga: New Moon*. He receives the Teen Choice Award for Fresh Face Male for his role in *Twilight*. He is nominated for the MTV Movie Award for Best Breakthrough Performance Male for *Twilight*.

2010 He plays the part of Willy in *Valentine's Day* and Jacob Black in *The Twilight Saga: Eclipse*. He lands roles in the films *Stretch Armstrong; Abduction; Cancun; Max Steel; Northern Lights;* and *The Twilight Saga: Breaking Dawn*. He is nominated for a People's Choice Award for the Favorite Breakout Movie Actor and Favorite On-Screen Team with Robert Pattinson and Kristen Stewart for their roles in *Twilight*.

FILMOGRAPHY

2010 *The Twilight Saga: Eclipse*
Valentine's Day
2009 *The Twilight Saga: New Moon*
2008 *My Own Worst Enemy* (TV; 7 episodes)
Twilight
2006 *He's a Bully, Charlie Brown* (voice)
Love, Inc. (TV; 1 episode)
2005 *Cheaper by the Dozen 2*
Danny Phantom (TV; voice; 3 episodes)
Duck Dodgers (TV; voice; 2 episodes)
The Adventures of Sharkboy and Lavagirl 3-D
What's New, Scooby-Doo? (TV; voice; 2 episodes)
2004 *My Wife and Kids* (TV; 1 episode)
The Bernie Mac Show (TV; 2 episodes)
Summerland (TV; 1 episode)
The Nick & Jessica Variety Hour (TV)
2001 *Shadow Fury*

FIND OUT MORE

Articles
Scarola, Danielle, and Patricia McNamara. "GL What's Hot." *Girls' Life*, December 2009/January 2010, Vol. 16 Issue 3, pp. 42–44.

Works Consulted
Carter, Kelly L. "This Happens Once in a 'New Moon.'" *USA Today*, November 17, 2009.

Hamilton, Terri Finch. "Actor, Teen Heartthrob Taylor Lautner Is in the 'Twilight' Zone." *The Grand Rapids Press*, October 12, 2008. http://www.mlive.com/living/grand-rapids/index.ssf/2008/10/profile_actor_teen_heartthrob.html

Hayes, Robert. "Jacob the Wolf." *Tribute*, October/November 2009, Vol. 26 Issue 6, pp. 28–29.

Martin, Michael. "Taylor Lautner." *Interview*, n.d., http://www.interviewmagazine.com/film/taylor-lautner/

Peretz, Evgenia. "Twilight's Hot Gleaming." *Vanity Fair*, December 2009, Issue 592, pp. 210–221.

Sherman, Kimberly. "Proof that New Moon's Taylor Lautner is Actually a 17 Year Old Boy. *Examiner*. July 17, 2009.

Sperling, Nicole. "The Twilight Saga: New Moon." *Entertainment Weekly*. August 21, 2009, pp. 34–39.

Strauss, Neil. "Teen Wolf." *Rolling Stone*, December 10, 2009, Issue 1093, pp. 54–61.

Videos
Exclusive Interview with Taylor Lautner
  http://www.youtube.com/watch?v=V_QvBnHGIeM

Kristen Stewart and Taylor Lautner Interview Comic-Con 2009
  http://www.youtube.com/watch?v=NCGofbBPbt0

Taylor Lautner Interview for *The Twilight Saga: New Moon*
  http://www.youtube.com/watch?v=VbGHBTHo8Dk

Taylor Lautner's Interview on DIRECTV's 4th Annual Celebrity Beach Bowl
  http://www.youtube.com/watch?v=aB9MgLS9IZs

PHOTO CREDITS: Cover, pp. 1, 3–Evans Ward/AP Photo; pp. 4, 6–Michael Tran/FilmMagic/GettyImages; p. 8–Barry King/WireImage/GettyImages; pp. 11, 23–Jeff Kravitz/FilmMagic/GettyImages; p. 12–S. Granitz/WireImage/GettyImages; pp. 14, 18–CreativeCommons; p. 21–Casey Rodgers/WireImage/GettyImages; p. 24–Maury Phillips/WireImage/GettyImages. Every effort has been made to locate all copyright holders of materials used in this book. Any errors or omissions will be corrected in future editions of the book.

GLOSSARY

audition (aw-DIH-shun)—A short performance given by an actor to try to get a part in a production.

Comic-Con International (in-ter-NASH-uh-nul)—The largest comic book and popular arts convention in the world.

commercial (kuh-MER-shul) **airline**—A company that transports passengers on airplanes.

commuting (kuh-MYOO-ting)—Traveling back and forth from your home to your work or school.

confidence (KON-fih-dunts)—Feeling sure about your abilities, qualities, or ideas.

convention (kun-VEN-shun)—A large meeting of an organization or political group.

discipline (DIH-suh-plin)—The ability to behave in a strictly controlled way.

hyperventilator (hy-per-VEN-tih-lay-tur)—A person who breathes very fast, losing control of his or her breathing.

morph (MORF)—To change into something else.

paparazzi (pah-pah-RAHT-zee)—Photographers who follow famous people, hoping to take photographs they can sell.

sequel (SEE-kwul)—The next in a series of movies, books, or events.

transform (trans-FORM)—To change into something else.

INDEX

Abduction 27
Adventures of Sharkboy and Lavagirl 3D, The 14, 16–17
Books for Kids Foundation 27
Breaking Dawn 27
Cancun 27
Celebrity Beach Bowl 11
Chat, Mike 13, 15
Cheaper by the Dozen 2 8, 17
Comic-Con International 4, 5–7, 22
Dooley, Taylor 14
Eclipse 27
Fabiano, Tom 12
Fabiano's Karate 11
Grand Rapids, Michigan 9
Holland, Michigan 11
Hudgens, Vanessa Anne 24
Hudsonville, Michigan 10
Jamestown Elementary 10
Karate 11, 12, 13, 15, 17
Lautner, Deb (mother) 9, 10, 25
Lautner, Daniel (father) 9, 10, 25
Lautner, Makena (sister) 8, 9
Lautner, Taylor
 birth of 9
 and charities 11, 24, 26–27
 education of 9–10, 13, 17
 grandparents of 16, 26
 heritage of 19
 hobbies of 26
 as Jacob Black 6, 7, 18–19, 20, 21, 27
 religion of 25
 and sports 10–11
Lollipop Theater Network 24, 25
Los Angeles, California 13, 15–16, 26
Martin, Steve 17
Max Steel 27
Michigan 9–11, 15, 25
New Moon 5–7, 20, 21, 22
New York Jets 11
Paparazzi 22, 26
Pattinson, Robert 6, 7
Quileute 19–20
Sanchez, Mark 11
San Diego Convention Center 5
Stewart, Kristen 6
Stretch Armstrong 27
Swift, Taylor 14
Tailor Made Entertainment 27
Team Chat International 13
Twilight 4, 5–7, 18, 19–20, 21, 22–23
Valentine's Day 14
Weitz, Chris 21–22